A   ıter

Conner Jones

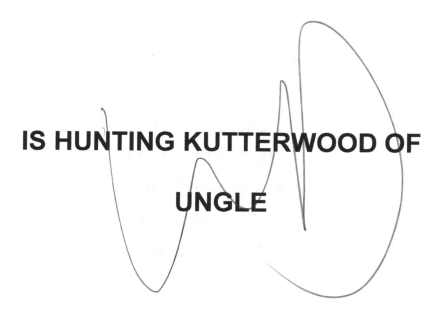

IS HUNTING KUTTERWOOD OF

UNGLE

Follow Conner Jones on his other Hunts:

1. Snorflag of Lavaton
2. Kutterwood of Ungle
3. Glayciar of Eyce
4. Shatter of Krystal
5. Warter of Layquid
6. Lology of Fless
7. Gass of Vaypoor
8. Durst of Zand
9. Shift of Tyme
10. Eyon of Metron

THE UNIVERSE OF THE ALIEN HUNTERS

You've probably not met an alien before.

(If you have report it to the police straight away)

If you haven't then you've never heard of some of

the alien races you will read about in this book. Take

care to study and learn. You never know when you

might be called upon to hunt some aliens.

It's best to be prepared.

THE JUDGES OF THE UNIVERSE

In order to police and ensure peace throughout the whole of existence, the **Judges of the Universe** were created.

They write the laws of the cosmos and ensure they are kept by all.

Any civilised planet may request that they be protected by the Judges. They will then help that civilisation safeguard their world.

The enforcement arm of the Judges are millions of Guard Robots, built to track criminals and capture them for the Judges. The robots are loyal and bound by their circuits to carry out their duty, without hesitation or fear.

GUARD ROBOTS

The Guard Robots are capable of capturing any alien from any planet in the known universe. They are strong and intelligent, with few weaknesses.

GUARD ROBOT NO. 3672

One of the oldest robots, with many years of experience that many new Guard Robots seek to download and learn from.

However he is so old now that repairing him is very costly. He no longer tracks and captures alien criminals any more. Instead he transports prisoners across the galaxy for the Judges.

THE ALIEN HUNTERS

CONNER JONES: A natural adventurer, often exploring the forest near his home. If there is a chance to do something exciting Conner will leap at the opportunity.

ELISE ROBERTS: One of the most compassionate people you will ever meet, always eager to help people in need. Her dream is to become a doctor when she's older.

LUKE EVANS: No one is keener on space than Luke Evans and he hopes to actually go there as an astronaut one day. He's a clever boy and usually able to outsmart his best friend Conner.

THE TEN WORST CRIMINALS IN THE UNIVERSE

The Top Ten are a collection of the most vile, traitorous, mad, evil criminals in the universe. They all have many, many crimes to their names. One managed to forge an empire ruling over two whole galaxies. Another stole all the treasures in the Nebula Bank on Valisner 8. Three have committed such horrid crimes that records of their existence have been wiped from all known databases. Currently they are being transported to the penal facility on Bling Blab 7, an inescapable prison guarded by Space Dogs.

KUTTERWOOD OF UNGLE

Height – No upper limit recorded

Skin Colour – Almost always green

Age – 53

Number of Limbs – No upper limit recorded

Kutterwood committed her first crime at the age of 16, when she broke into the Thousand World Art Collection on the Mucla asteroid.

She didn't steal anything, just spent all night viewing the paintings after swallowing the guards.

At the age of 49 she stole the plans for the Torpor Contain from its holy resting place.

She loves all things shiny and unique.

As a member of the Unglian species, Kutterwood is a plant like organism requiring sunlight and water to keep herself nourished. She is capable of transforming any landscape into a steamy jungle full of carnivorous plants.

ALIEN TECHNOLOGY

Spear - Conner was given a Spear to use against the alien criminals. It fires Blue Energy ropes to tie up the aliens.

Shield – Elise received a Shield that can produce a bubble of Red Energy to protect herself and others from the aliens.

Gauntlets – Luke received a pair of Gauntlets that glow with Green Energy, giving enhanced speed and the ability to stick to any surface.

All these weapons can also be summoned back to their owners by Mental Control

The Prison Ship

Guard Robot No. 3672 (who the Alien Hunters call Mach, short for Machine), transports his alien criminals through space in a large vessel equipped with weapons, prison cells and a cargo bay for transporting dangerous aliens and dangerous objects. It is shaped like a whale.

The Galaxy Wing

The Galaxy Wing is a small alien space ship. It is shaped like a shark. The Alien Hunters use the Galaxy Wing to chase down the Aliens.

13

PROLOGUE

Paris, probably the most famous city in the entire world! That was what Philippe thought as he marvelled at its buildings and streets from on top of the *Arc de Triomphe*, a magnificent arch built by the famous Napoleon Bonaparte.

The *Arc*, perhaps the centre piece of the French capital city, was a monument to its greatness. It offered unrivalled views of the *Champs-Élysées*, a majestic boulevard of shops.

Philippe was a security guard at the *Arc* and he loved to go onto the roof of the building late at night and view his city.

Because of his love for the building, he took his duties as guard very seriously. He was well trained in keeping kids from spilling their soft drinks all over the polished stone. He also excelled at shouting at them when they dared to cross the velvet red ropes that cordoned off certain areas.

It was his duty to protect the magnificent structure and protect it he shall.

He left the roof and performed his rounds on the upper level of the *Arc*, and then he took the stairs down to the security office. He admired the artwork on display inside the *Arc* and the busts of heroes carved into the arched roof.

He came to a sudden halt when he saw a woman standing on the stairwell. She was admiring the building and had her back to him. Philippe swelled his chest and straightened his back. He looked forward to these moments when he got to exert some authority.

His shoes made loud purposeful steps as he descended the stairs down to the woman. He saw that she was dressed in a long overcoat with the collar pointing up and covering her neck. A large wide brimmed hat kept her head from view.

"Excuse me madam, the *Arc* is closed for the evening and you should not be here," he said.

There was no response from the woman. The only sound coming from her was a faint rustling, like dry leaves.

Philippe raised his hand and placed it on the woman's shoulder.

"You have to…" he began and stopped mid - sentence when he felt her shoulder.

Something seemed to be writhing underneath her coat, it felt like hundreds of snakes.

Philippe stepped back as the woman turned towards him.

"Yes it will do nicely," she said.

Philippe took his Nightstick, a foot long tube of metal, from his belt. He held it aloft, ready to strike. "What are you?" he said in terror, when he saw what was beneath the coat.

The woman didn't answer.

Vines suddenly sprung from within her clothing and enveloped the guard, forcing him towards the far wall and holding him there. His nightstick clattered to the floor, useless against his foe.

The vines snaked their way over the walls of the *Arc*. One found a drinks fountain and pried it off the wall.

Water gushed out onto the floor and the vines soaked themselves, growing quickly as they drank in the liquid.

As the plants spread from the woman she raised her arms and laughed.

"Finally, a city that will be mine...forever."

THE SUMMONS

Conner sat at his school desk in his classroom with his head resting on his hands. His eyes were un-focused as he stared at the teacher who wrote sums on the board.

Although he was there in body, his mind was wandering far away.

He was thinking about Luke Evans his best friend. Two days ago he, Luke and Elise, another of his friends, had discovered an alien space ship in the forest near his house.

Inside had been a robot, who Conner had named Mach, that had been guarding ten of the universe's worst alien criminals. One had escaped, a being called Snorflag of Lavaton, a creature made from living lava.

Because of the damage to his ship and his robotic body, the machine had asked Conner, Luke and Elise to hunt down the alien, and return him to his ship.

They succeeded.

Luke however had been brainwashed during that adventure and forced to help the rest of the criminals the robot guarded, to escape.

Then he had disappeared.

Conner wished that he could see his friend again.

But Luke had not been seen for the last couple of days, he hadn't even returned home and Mach, Conner's name for the robot guard, had not had any luck in finding him.

Conner also wasn't entirely happy with how they covered up Luke's disappearance. Mr and Mrs Evans were great people, however the only way to excuse Luke's absence had been to fool them into believing that Luke was on a few weeks holiday, visiting distant relatives. This had been achieved through using the same brainwashing technology Snorflag had used on Luke. Mach had used it to convince them *they* had sent their son away on the holiday. Their school was not happy with his absence, but Mach had apparently taken care of that too, Conner didn't know how.

"Mr Jones will you sit up straight," his teacher said and Conner, surprised at being addressed so suddenly while his thoughts were elsewhere, jerked awkwardly in his seat. The whole class laughed at his antics.

The teacher ignored the laughter and strode across the classroom and stood before Conner's desk.

She breathed in deeply - no doubt preparing a lengthy speech.

Conner gripped the edge of his desk and looked up at her in terror.

Just then the school's intercom system came on and the headmaster's voice blared out across the school. "Coonner Jones, Connnner Jonessss pleasssse reportttt to the headmaster's officcce immediately," he said. His voice was oddly slurred and Conner's fellow pupils sniggered at the bizarre transmission.

His teacher's shoulders sagged and she frowned. She was now unable to deliver her tirade at him.

Conner's chair screeched as he pushed back away from his desk and set off for the headmaster's office, wondering what kind of

trouble he was in.

THE ROBOT DAD

Conner strolled up to the headmaster's office, in no hurry at all to face him, and looked through the window that ran down the length of it.

He saw the headmaster chatting to a huge person in a massive padded coat. Conner didn't recognise him.

The headmaster didn't look cross though so Conner assumed that he wasn't in trouble, this was about something else.

He knocked on the door and the headmaster beckoned him in.

"Ah Conner your daaaaad is here to take yooouuu out of schoollll for the rest of the daaaay," the headmaster said, in the same slurred manner of speaking as his broadcast. He also indicated toward the giant sitting in front of him.

The giant of a man turned around and Conner saw that it was Mach, who was wearing glasses that ill fitted his robotic eyes. He also wore a hat that had been squeezed onto his head, tearing

its sides.

Conner looked at the headmaster - then back to

the robot who smiled.

"This is my dad?" he asked the headmaster.

"Of course it is boy, don't you recognise him?"

The headmaster looked at the nine foot tall robot

and didn't see anything wrong with this scenario.

Mach looked straight at him, "come on son we

have to go," he said.

Conner stared at the robot. One of the lights

behind his eyes flickered on and off, Conner was

sure that the robot had just winked at him.

This is about one of the escaped aliens, Conner thought, *it was time to go to work and hunt them and more importantly - maybe find Luke as well.*

"Yeah dad I'm ready to go," Conner said and nodded.

"Ok you two get going," he replied.

Conner led Mach out into the school grounds and through the school gates, once they were out of view, Conner turned to Mach.

"Dad?" he asked.

Mach pulled from his pocket something that looked like a can of air freshener, "this is called Disguise Spray, it makes people see what I want them to see."

"So the headmaster thought he was looking at my dad? Why was he talking in such a weird way?"

"A side effect. Sorry but this Disguise Spray is the only way I could get into the school and get you out," Mach answered.

"Why the coat, hat and glasses?"

"Sometimes it's necessary to help the disguise along with clothing belonging to the person you intend to imitate. Now..." he began, taking off the hat and forcing a blond wig onto his head, "...time to impersonate Elise's Mum and get her out of school too." The robot turned around and headed back to the building.

Conner did his best not to laugh.

THE PLANT

After rescuing Elise from a history class they all returned to the forest where Mach's Prison Ship lay half buried in the mud.

Because the ship had crashed with such speed it had dug itself into the earth with tremendous force. Trees were still standing on top of it, their roots cascading down the flanks of the ship reaching for the soil.

Surrounding it were poles that encircled the entire vessel. The circle was the width of a football stadium.

"What are those for?" Conner asked Mach.

"They ward off any humans that try to approach the ship, they're called Mind Dampeners and they cause humans to simply change their minds and do the opposite of what they intended to do," Mach explained. "So if someone wanted to investigate this part of the forest they would change their minds and go somewhere else as soon as they were in range of the dampeners."

"Why aren't we affected?" Elise asked.

"I've tuned them to allow you two to approach the ship," Mach said.

They entered his vessel and strolled down the central corridor.

They passed by nine open doors and one sealed door.

Conner saw that it was bolted shut and secured with various locks. He was glad to see such security, after all Snorflag of Lavaton was inside that cell and Conner remembered how dangerous he was.

Mach stopped at the door and pushed a button next to it. Conner heard a splash of water from inside. "A daily dose of water keeps Snorflag rock solid," Mach explained.

After entering the Control Centre Conner sat in one of the chairs, as did Elise. Mach then went and pressed a few buttons on a console and displayed on a nearby screen was an image of an alien.

"Behold Kutterwood of Ungle," he said, "she is your next target."

Conner and Elise stared at the representation of Kutterwood. She was in essence a giant plant. Much of her body was big and bulbous like a pitcher plant, a carnivorous plant. Various leaves and vines grew from the top of her body like hair and roots formed a base that held her upright. She had no face - instead a set of markings on her body made it look like she had eyes.

"Kutterwood is a thief," Mach explained, "but she doesn't steal for profit, she steals to own what she takes. She also doesn't care who she harms to get what she wants. She once stole a piece of Maldainium, a rare metal that was the key to maintaining the power supply of an entire planet. That world suffered because she robbed them of the means to keep the lights on, maintain hospital equipment and their economy."

"How was she caught?" Elise said.

"Ten Guard Robots were able to cut off her roots and limbs depriving her of water, without it she reverts to a seedling," Mach said.

"So where is she?" Conner said, eager to get going, because if he found her maybe he would find Luke too.

"I have tracked her to a city called Paris," Mach

said.

Elise smiled, "I've always wanted to go to Paris."

"Not so far away then," Conner commented.

"The distance is not what concerns me," Mach

replied.

"How come?" Conner asked.

"Because Paris is where she could do the most

damage."

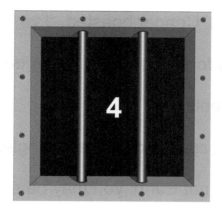

THE MISSION

"Why Paris?" Elise said.

"In terms of precious gems, artwork, architecture, sculptures, monuments - it's a treasure trove and that means Kutterwood is going to try and steal as much of it as possible," Mach said. "You must get there soon and stop her. She's an Unglian so that means she can transform the environment around her to resemble a jungle or forest."

"No problem," Conner boasted, "I've lived all my life near this forest, I'm used to a wide variety of trees and plants."

"But she can create forests and jungles from her home-world, not Earth; you may be surprised by some very different plants and trees."

Conner and Elise absorbed this information. Conner then asked the question he had been waiting to ask for ages.

"Any sign of Luke?" he said.

"I have no way of tracking him, but he might be in Paris with Kutterwood," Mach suggested.

"How are we going to break his brainwashing?" Elise asked.

"We can't undo it, but there is another solution," Mach said and he brought the brainwasher Snorflag had built out of a nearby safe in the Control Centre. It was a device cobbled together from Human technology such as laptops, phones and calculators.

"All we have to do is re-program this to brainwash Luke to revert to his old self," Mach explained.

"First we have to catch him and he's got a teleporter and those gauntlets," Elise said.

Conner had forgotten about the gauntlets. He Elise and Luke had each received alien weapons from Mach to assist them in capturing aliens. Luke's chosen weapon allowed him to move very fast. The teleporter could also send him anywhere within 10,000 miles, and also told their users when someone else was teleporting nearby.

"Yes it will be difficult, but I know that you can do it and restore your friend," Mach said.

Conner and Elise looked at each other and nodded in agreement. They had vowed to one another to do everything they could to get their best friend back.

"There is one more thing," Mach added.

"What?" Conner replied.

"Kutterwood's last crime was to steal plans for a device called the Torpor Contain," Mach explained. "It is essentially an inescapable prison, which creates a force-field that is impenetrable, similar to the force-field Elise's shield produces, only more powerful. Depending on how much energy you can charge it with, depends on how big it will be and how long the force-field will last. Be careful Kutterwood may have one in her possession, you don't want to get imprisoned yourself do you?"

"No we don't," Elise said.

Conner agreed, the thought of being locked up scared him.

He then smiled when he realised how they were going to get to Paris.

"Well then let's get on board the Galaxy Wing and get going," Conner said, rushing off for the launch bay.

THE BIRD

The Galaxy Wing shot out of the Prison Ship and into the skies above England at terrific speed.

"Yahooooo," Conner yelled feeling elated to be back at the controls of the ship again.

A small screen extended from the ceiling displaying Mach's face.

"Because you're flying in day time and further than before, you should activate the ship's Cloaking Field," the robot said.

Conner's eyes lit up, "you mean we're going to make the ship go invisible?" he asked.

"No," Mach replied.

"Oh."

"The Cloaking Field projects an image out from the hull of the Galaxy Wing so that people on the outside will not see a ship at all. I'm setting it to project the image of a bird that lives on the planet Earth."

"What's the bird?" Elise said.

"You call it an eagle and the image will reset every time you take off and land."

"So whenever someone looks at the ship they'll see an eagle?" Elise asked.

"Yes," Mach replied.

"Cool," Conner said.

"Activating it now," Mach said.

Conner, smiling in excitement, looked out of the window. He didn't see any change to the ship though.

"It's not working, nothing has changed."

"We won't notice the difference from inside the ship," Elise said.

"Oh yeah – right," Conner muttered.

He flew the Wing from their village towards the coast of England. "Which way to Paris?" he asked.

"Keep going straight you're heading in the right direction," Elise said, consulting a computer. Conner looked over his shoulder and saw her reading more information.

"What are you reading?" he asked.

"It's information about Paris," she said.

"You don't need to do that, we're not going to be there for long," Conner said.

"Conner it's best to know something about where we're going, and be prepared for whatever we might have to deal with," Elise said, scolding him.

"I've been to France on holiday before, I know all I need to know," he said.

Elise looked at the back of his head and

mouthed the word *idiot*.

"Whatever you say Conner, whatever you say,"

she said out loud.

THE TRACKER

After ten minutes of flight time Elise reported on their progress.

"I've got the signal from the tracker it seems to be by the Eiffel Tower," Elise said.

The Galaxy Wing soared over the capital of France, over the Louvre and the River Seine as Conner piloted it towards the giant tower that dominated the city's skyline.

"Wow look at that thing, it's impressive," Elise commented. "Did you know that two million rivets hold it together, my computer says so?"

"Whatever," was all Conner could say and Elise rolled her eyes. "Where is Kutterwood?" Conner asked.

The area around the tower was decorated with various plants and trees and Conner wondered if the alien was hiding amongst them.

There were numerous stalls around the tower and some of them were selling flowers, making Conner even more nervous.

"We need to land," Elise said.

"Yeah," Conner agreed, "but this is a public area. People will see us."

"Well we look like a bird maybe we should land in a tree," Elise suggested.

Conner thought about it and realised that it wasn't a bad idea.

He manoeuvred the ship above a very large tree and used the strong branches to support the ship as he shut down the engines.

Conner looked out of the window to see if anyone could see them.

A few people were pointing at them, but they weren't shocked, merely curious.

"Let's go," Conner said.

He and Elise exited the Galaxy Wing, grabbing their weapons as they left, and stepped out onto the tree and climbed down to the ground.

Conner glanced back up at the ship and saw instead a very large eagle perched on top of the high branches.

"Wow! That Cloaking Field works brilliantly," he said.

Elise looked around at the French people, they too appeared to see the eagle, and many of them stared in curiosity at its appearance in their city. "It has them fooled."

The last few branches down and out of the tree were a bit of a struggle and both Conner and Elise lost their footing and fell from the tree.

A smattering of leaves followed them down, falling like snow.

There were some French mutterings at their sudden appearance.

A policeman strolled up to the pair of them and hauled them to their feet.

"Tu viens d'ou?" he said to them.

"Pardon?" Conner said, deciding to adopt a French accent to help himself blend in.

"Ah English tourist," the Frenchman said. "No climbing the trees, now go to your parents," he said and wandered off.

"That was close we were almost arrested," Conner said. "Let's hurry up and find this alien, the onboard computer said the signal was coming from under the tower."

They both headed for the tower. Nothing seemed to be out of the ordinary, despite the fact that an alien was out in the open. The tourists were clamouring for the stairs and lifts to go up the tower, people were taking photographs, citizens of the city went about their business.

It was normal, everyday life.

"Surely someone should have spotted this alien by now," Conner said, as he and Elise both reached the underside of the tower. Above them were hundreds of people with lots of eyes that could spot an alien, however there was no panic or alarm, the alien wasn't there.

"Oh dear," Elise said looking at the ground.

"What?" Conner said.

He followed her gaze to something lying on the floor. It was small tube, like a battery, and covered with a purple liquid.

"I think that's the tracker," Elise said.

Conner bent down and picked it up. It had alien writing down its side, "it's not human that's for sure, we won't be able to find Kutterwood without her being attached to this."

"Hello guys," someone said in English behind them.

Conner recognised the voice instantly and turned sharply to see Luke standing ten meters from them.

"Luke!" Elise blurted out in surprise.

"Hello," Luke repeated.

Conner took in his appearance and noticed something seemed off about Luke.

He wore a massive smile, as if being brainwashed and missing for the last two days seemed like a non event. He was still wearing his gauntlets and for some reason he was carrying a long bundle of very thick cables. He was also extremely dirty; mud caked his trousers and shoes.

"Mate it's good to see you," Conner said.

"It's good to see you too," Luke replied still smiling.

"Look mate we need to get you back to the Prison Ship so Mach can help you," Conner said.

"Nah sorry I can't do that," Luke replied, "I have a job to do," and he indicated the cables he held.

"Luke please," Elise pleaded.

"I also like working for these aliens I've done some very cool stuff over these last couple days," Luke boasted.

Conner very slowly positioned his spear so that he could fire an energy net at Luke.

Suddenly Luke was gone. "You can't catch me," he said from behind them.

Conner remembered that his gauntlets gave him the power to move really fast and he had a teleporter. Conner had to admit that he probably wasn't going to be fast enough to catch Luke.

"Besides I can't leave I have to make sure the trap works," Luke said.

"What trap?" Conner said.

"This one," he said, then he reached into his pocket and pulled out a bottle of water. He took the lid off and threw it at Conner's feet.

The bottle leaked water onto the ground.

"What the..?" Elise said.

Then the ground exploded as huge vines erupted from under the turf, ensnaring Elise and Conner.

THE FLORIST

Conner felt vines wrap around his waist and legs.

There were screams and shouts from nearby people and all of them rushed to get away from the fast growing vines.

Conner activated his spear and shot energy nets at any of the thin rope-like plants he could aim at.

The nets worked very well and the vines got tangled in them. However they were growing fast and replacing those that Conner managed to subdue.

Elise was safe from the plants, her shield had extended a bubble around her, and the vines were unable to penetrate it. She was trapped though, unable to help Conner without turning her shield off.

And Conner really needed help. He was being raised high into the air by the vines. His nets couldn't handle the huge number of plants.

So instead he sent out a long rope of energy towards one of the legs of the Eiffel Tower.

The rope stuck to one of the lifts that was rising up to the first level of the tower. As he held onto his spear Conner was pulled away from the vines by the rising elevator. Soon he was dangling over the plants that flayed around beneath him.

Conner threw his legs backwards and forwards, extended the rope he held onto, and swung himself out of reach of the vines.

Elise burst out of the web of flora in her sphere of energy, she ran towards him and turned off her shield.

The plant started wrapping itself around the tower, searching for fresh targets.

"What are we going to do?" she said, "that thing is still growing."

"I can help."

Elise and Conner were approached by a boy who had been standing near a flower stall, one of many encircling the tower. He wore an apron stained green and a classical French beret on his head, which restrained a mess of black hair.

"What?" Conner said.

"I can help," the boy repeated.

"No you need to stay back - this is dangerous," Conner said.

"Dangerous, I am ten years old," the boy said.

"How can you help?" Elise asked.

"I know all about plants, if you want to stop this one you need to attack its core not the vines. Look I have some weed killer with me, douse it onto the core and it will die," the boy said.

"Weed killer takes ages to affect plants," Conner said.

"No it won't, this is my own special recipe, it will kill weeds in seconds," the boy boasted.

Elise and Conner looked at each other. Mach had told not to tell others about aliens, however they needed the boy's help.

"Alright then here's the plan, I'll distract it while Elise will get you to the vine's core inside her shield," Conner said.

"Oui," the boy said.

"What?"

"Yes," the boy replied patiently.

"Go," Conner said, and he rushed off whipping the vines of the plant with his spear which sought him out. He weaved his staff around chopping the ends of the vines off and sending more nets to hold off the ones that got too close.

He watched as Elise and the boy surrounded themselves with the shield bubble and pushed their way through the vines to the core.

But they were soon having trouble, the vines were very thick near the centre of the plant and hard to get through. Conner wasn't distracting them enough and needed to make himself a better target. He then sent the longest rope he had ever produced out above the vines to a girder on the underside of the tower. He then reeled it in and leapt into the air, swinging out over the plant that sent all of its 'limbs' up to try and catch him.

That gave Elise and the boy the break they needed and swiftly they reached the core of the vines. Elise turned off her shield and they both fell into the mass of plant life, pouring the weed killer on top of the plant as they dived into its exact centre.

As soon as the liquid touched the plant it suffered a violent spasm, throwing Elise and the boy away from it.

The weed killer did its job.

The plant suddenly went limp.

Its vines turned brown.

Eventually it shrivelled up until it was just a pile

of rotting compost.

"Yay." Elise said weakly, punching the air in

triumph, and then collapsing from exhaustion.

THE POWER

Conner breathed a sigh of relief and lowered himself down to the ground.

He joined Elise and the boy who were shaken, but unhurt.

"Well done...what was your name?" Conner asked the boy.

"My name is Peter," the boy said.

"That was good stuff," Conner said, admiring the empty bottle of weed killer that lay on top of the remains of the vines, which was now just a pile of mulch.

"It should be, I created it," the boy said, "now tell me what's going on here?" he asked.

Conner looked at Elise, she shook her head, "we can't tell you," he answered.

"Look an alien just attacked the Eiffel Tower in my city and I want to know why," Peter said.

"You knew it was alien?" Conner asked.

"Not for sure, but you just confirmed it," Peter said smiling.

Conner glared at Peter.

"Calm down Conner," Elise said. "Peter, the boy who was here before, what was he doing?"

"I saw him come out of that building there," Peter said. He pointed towards a structure not far away. "It's the control room for the tower."

Conner looked over and saw that the door to the building was wide open.

"We need to check it out," Conner said.

Elise and Conner wandered over to the building, Peter followed them.

"Go away," Conner said to the boy.

"No way, I want to know what's going on," Peter said.

Conner shot a net of energy at Peter, which wrapped the boy up and he fell to the floor.

"Hey," the boy shouted.

"Conner!" Elise chided him

"What? We can't have him getting in danger," Conner said, and he and Elise continued on towards the building with Peter shouting after them.

They entered the building cautiously. Inside were switches and dials all recording and monitoring power. There were numerous lightning bolt symbols so Conner concluded that this room specifically controlled the electricity going into the Eiffel Tower.

"Why was Luke in here?" he asked.

"I think he's doing something to the power, look," Elise said and she indicated thick electric cables that snaked into the floor. Some had been re-routed or cut and fused altogether. Conner remembered that Luke had been holding some power cables when they had first seen him.

"Why does he need power?" Conner said.

"No idea," Elise replied.

Suddenly from outside there was a gigantic boom and they heard the distant noise of screams and shouts.

Conner and Elise rushed outside and looked around for the source of the commotion.

On the horizon, across the Seine, huge plants were growing and flowering, more vines also writhed and wrapped around the buildings.

"It's Kutterwood, she's changing the environment," Elise said, "just like Snorflag."

"Where is that?" Conner said.

"That is the *Arc de Triomphe*," Peter answered, who was still struggling inside his net.

Conner deactivated the energy net and Peter stood up, looking at the horizon in shock.

"We're being invaded again," he said.

"Again?" Conner asked.

"My grandfather, he told me about the occupation during World War Two, it's happening again," Peter said.

"This isn't war," Conner said.

"We need to get there," Elise said and she and

Conner headed towards where they had parked

the Galaxy Wing.

"I'm coming with you," Peter cried out.

Conner shot another net at the boy and left him

sprawled on the ground.

Peter cursed him in French all the way to the

spaceship.

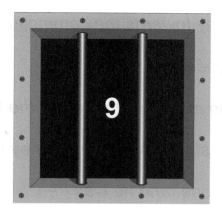

THE WEED KILLER

Peter struggled in the bonds the English boy had shot at him.

He wondered how this was possible, for energy to trap him like this and for light to be solid.

Then he heard the sound of someone starting up a jet engine and he squirmed onto his side and saw a falcon lift off from the top of a nearby tree *and soar away towards the commotion on the*

Champs-Élysées.

As the falcon moved further away the bonds that

bound Peter started to fade until they were

completely gone, and he was free.

He sat on the ground underneath the tower in

awe of the chaos around him.

The plants growing in the centre of the city had

people running for their lives.

It was just like the stories his grandfather had

told him, Paris was being invaded therefore there

needed to be a resistance.

Peter watched as people ran about in terror like

pigs who had figured out where bacon comes

from. He went to his flower stall ignoring the

adults as they cowered from the uproar in the centre of the city.

Having witnessed firsthand the effects of his home-made weed killer, Peter decided to make more and immediately started cooking up another batch, only this time he was going to make it more potent than ever.

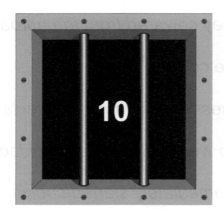

THE CANNON PLANT

Conner lifted the Galaxy Wing from off the tree he had parked it in.

"Elise I think you're going to have to take control of the weapons and not the defences," Conner suggested.

Elise nodded and switched places. With some hesitation she sat in Luke's spot.

Mach's face appeared on one of the screens as soon as the ship powered up.

"What's happening? Why are you inflight again?"

"The tracker led us into a trap, but we've located Kutterwood regardless," Conner said.

He manoeuvred the Galaxy Wing from the tree they had parked it in and piloted it towards the jungle that was being formed in the centre of Paris.

"You need to be careful, the entire jungle is at her command just like Snorflag's volcano in the shopping centre," Mach said.

"They're just plants," Conner said.

"Alien plants," Mach emphasised.

"I'll be careful," Conner replied. Mach's face disappeared and Conner turned round to Elise, "ready?" he asked.

"Ready," came the reply.

Conner was glad she was, because he wasn't. To get near and land the Galaxy Wing close to Kutterwood was going to take some really good piloting, which he might not be capable of.

The ship flew over Paris and the twisting vines at the *Arc de Triomphe* grew closer. Several roads branched off from the *Arc* and all were being overrun with strange plants.

"We need to land somewhere," Conner said.

"I bet the *Arc* is covered in foliage by now so we won't be able to land on top of it," Elise said.

Suddenly blue lights began to flash on and off all around them.

"What does that mean?" Elise said.

"I don't know," Conner replied, "but it's blue light so it cannot be anything dangerous," he added, "Blue is a calming colour."

It was then that the Galaxy Wing was struck on its belly and the entire vessel lurched in the air. Conner had to wrestle with the controls.

"What was that?" he called out.

"We were fired at from the *Arc*," Elise said.

"By what?"

"A plant."

One of the computers then displayed an image of the plant. It was shaped like a half open rose, only its petals seemed a lot thicker. The plant twisted on its stalk until it was facing them and then the petals moved over each other, constricting and at the same time launching a projectile at them.

Conner swung the ship to the left and the projectile sailed past.

"We've got incoming," Elise said.

"Fire back please," Conner ordered, who now had to struggle with the controls of the ship to avoid all the vegetation being fired at him.

Elise tapped some buttons and the Galaxy Wing shuddered as it fired weapons. Conner couldn't see the weapons from inside the ship but he could watch the plants explode.

Various images on the screen showed other plants returning fire. When the Galaxy Wing's weapons destroyed them, new plants just grew in their place.

"This isn't working," Elise said. "What's that?" she cried out, pointing at a screen.

The display showed a new massive plant growing under the *Arc*. It was shaped like a giant un-opened tulip. The bell shaped plant started to swell and then spat a giant glob of liquid towards the Galaxy Wing.

Conner tried to dodge it but the blob was too big and it enveloped the ship.

The view screens went off line immediately, they were flying blind.

"We're going down," Conner said, as the engines

also went dark.

They could feel the ship descending and Conner

and Elise braced themselves for the inevitable

crash.

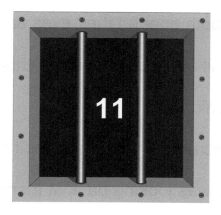

THE UNDERGROUND

The Galaxy Wing impacted the immaculate grass in the park next to the Eiffel Tower.

Its front end practically buried itself in the ground and the ship left a long trench in the turf.

Conner and Elise were still in their chairs their faces screwed up in fear, expecting the crash to be much worst.

When they both opened their eyes and saw that they were still alive. Conner said, "this is one tough little ship."

One of the screens then turned itself on and Mach's face was looking back at them.

"What happened? I detected a crash," he said.

"Yeah the ship's down," Conner said, "we just got blasted by a plant," he added.

"The ship is no good to you now, exit and I'll set the auto pilot to fly it home for repairs," Mach said.

"How do we get back?" Elise asked.

"Kutterwood still has a teleporter, use it to get home," Mach said.

"Let's go," Conner said and they both left the ship. When they got outside Conner was amazed at the damage to the park the landing had caused. He was even more amazed when he looked back at the ship and saw a swan sitting where the Wing was supposed to be. The cloaking system was still working.

When he and Elise were clear the swan made a heck of a lot of noise then took off into the sky heading back to the Prison Ship in England.

"Huh," Conner managed to say.

"What now?" Elise said.

"I guess we go on foot," Conner replied turning around and looking at the centre of Paris, now swamped with unfamiliar trees and plants.

"Don't you remember what *Redwater* was like? A whole building turned into a volcano. This time it's a jungle filled with deadly plants," Elise said.

"What else can we do?" Conner replied.

"I know a way," someone said.

They both spotted Peter standing at his flower stall nearby and pouring various liquids into bottles.

They both wandered over to him.

"You know a way over to the *Arc*?" Conner said.

Peter finished pouring and started screwing the tops onto the bottles he had filled.

"Yes a way that doesn't involve you going anywhere near plants," Peter added.

"Well where is it?" Conner said.

"First you have to promise to take me with you," Peter said.

Conner said, "no way, it's too dangerous."

"So dangerous that two eleven year olds are the only ones who can handle it?" Peter shot back.

"Two eleven years olds armed with powerful weapons," Conner said brandishing his spear.

"And I have my weapons," Peter said holding up his bottles that came complete with nozzles, allowing them to spray their liquid.

"What? Your orange squash?" Conner sneered.

"Deadly orange squash actually! This will kill weeds and plants faster than an English gardener," Peter replied.

Conner opened his mouth to reply but Elise stopped him.

"We need him Conner," Elise said.

Conner huffed, but shut his mouth and didn't say anything more.

"So Peter how do we do this?" Elise asked.

"Have you ever heard of the French Resistance?" Peter said.

"Yes I learnt about them in school," Conner replied.

"Well they used to move around the city undetected by using the sewers," he said.

"The sewers which are dirty and smelly," Conner pointed out.

"They also wind under the earth like worm tunnels, they aren't going to take us where we need to go," Elise said, then her eyes widened. "Actually they will," she realised.

"Because in Paris our sewers match the layout of the city above them," said Peter, voicing what she was thinking.

"How did you know that?" Conner asked Elise.

"I read remember," Elise replied, "you should have done the same. We can follow them to the *Arc* and Kutterwood wouldn't know we were coming," Elise said.

"Who's Kutterwood?" Peter asked.

"The enemy," Elise replied.

"So how do we get into the sewers?" Conner asked.

"Follow me," Peter said and they set off for the River Seine.

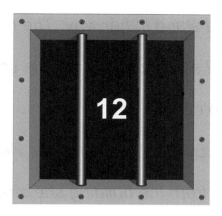

THE THORN WIRE

Kutterwood looked out over the city the humans called Paris.

She was thrilled to be here, out of all the cities on the planet this was the one she had chosen to steal. Because of its beauty and rare and valuable items.

Very soon it would all be hers.

No one could stand in her way. The robot guard

had tried and she had taken out his scout ship,

there was no danger now.

She looked down at the plants that were

creeping out from the building she stood on, they

were slowly encompassing the whole city. The

humans were running from them, as they should.

The plants were all growing from Kutterwood and

were all as dangerous as she was.

She saw one human female running away just

beneath her. Kutterwood spotted something

shiny around her neck.

She willed vines at the base of Arc to ensnare

her and strip her of the shiny things. The vines

let the woman go and she fled in terror,

screaming. The vines passed the shiny things all the way to Kutterwood.

"Hmm shiny rocks," Kutterwood said, then deposited the diamond necklace into her body for safe keeping.

The plants growing on the building then alerted her to the presence of someone behind her.

Only one human had not run - the one who had freed her, and Kutterwood turned her bulbous body around to face him.

The human was smiling, she thought that strange considering the things he had seen.

"Yes what is it?" she demanded.

"All the power conduits you wanted re-routed, have been, so what now?" Luke asked.

Kutterwood didn't congratulate him, she instead stared at his wrist.

"What's that?" she said seeing his watch.

"It's a watch?" he replied.

"I want it," she said admiring the way it ticked and shone.

Luke removed it and gave it to her.

"I want those gauntlets too," she said.

Luke smile faded and he backed off, "no way these are mine," he said.

Kutterwood was about to scream at him for his insolence. Everything should be hers, but she restrained her anger, she didn't have time for extra thieving.

"Very well, I have one last job for you."

"Yes," Luke said and his smile returned.

"You must defend this building until my plan is complete, then you can teleport away to help someone else," she said.

"No probs," the boy replied.

"Take this," Kutterwood prompted and handed him a plant.

The plant was basically the mouth of a Venus Fly trap. Its stalk was long and stretchy, connected to a system of roots, which latched onto Luke's wrist when he took it from Kutterwood.

"What is it?" Luke asked.

"A Thorn Wire it can grapple things to help you move about or seek out items you may wish to take from others, such as weapons," Kutterwood

explained. *"I want you to guard the building with it."*

"Sure thing," Luke replied and then wandered off admiring the Thorn Wire.

Kutterwood also left the roof and headed for the edifice's ground floor, dreaming of owning this city forever.

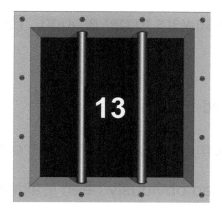

THE SMELL

Paris seemed strangely quiet as Conner, Elise and Peter, their new friend, walked along the banks of the Seine.

"My grandpapa used to be in the Resistance when he was my age. The Resistance used him to send messages across the city because the invaders wouldn't a suspect a child. Occasionally he used the sewers to get around," Peter explained.

"I'm so thrilled," Conner said.

Peter led them to a tunnel that was covered by a grill. Water had obviously been leaking out of it and into the Seine recently, as there was a stain leading from its base down into the river.

"We need to get the grill off," he stated, pointing towards the lock.

Conner lent forward and tried to pull at the grill, but the lock held fast.

"I don't have a key," he said.

"I've an idea," Elise said and stepped forward and wedged her shield between the grill and the tunnel wall.

She then activated the shield.

The red bubble it produced expanded from the shield and forced the grill away from the wall. The lock strained to keep it over the mouth of the tunnel entrance, but eventually it couldn't handle the pressure. The metal grid sprung away from the tunnel entrance, mangling the lock.

"Hold it right there," someone said to them.

A French policeman came striding towards them. "You children have to get away from here. What are you doing?" the policeman asked.

"We don't have time for this," Conner said and shot a net at the policeman from his spear, who collapsed as the energy bound him.

"What, what is this?" he cried out.

"Nice job," Peter said.

"If you like that you will love this," Conner said, and aimed the spear at Peter.

"Don't do it, you need me to guide you," Peter said.

Conner shoulders slumped, the boy was right.

"You first though," he said and pointed down the tunnel.

Peter smiled and headed underground followed by Elise and reluctantly - Conner.

●

"I am so glad you brought us down here," Conner said holding his nose in the dank dark tunnel. The only light illuminating their way was the blue light from the end of Conner's spear and what it revealed was awful.

"It's the only way to get to Kutterwood," Elise said.

"Who is this Kutterwood?" Peter said.

Elise looked over her shoulder at Conner, no doubt wondering if it was best to tell the boy about the alien criminals or not.

"I know it's an alien, but what is it doing in my city," Peter added.

Conner nodded to Elise.

"Kutterwood is a criminal from another planet, and we have to track her down and stop whatever it is she's here to do," Elise said.

"What about that other boy?" Peter said.

"He's a friend," Conner said quickly.

"Not a very good one," Peter pointed out.

Elise held up her hand to stop Conner from going for the French boy and said, "he was brainwashed to assist the alien, he can't help himself."

"Oh, sorry," Peter said.

"Thank you," Conner muttered.

Peter led them to a much wider tunnel where water flowed down it like a river. Strangely there was a jetty stretching out across the water and an old boat moored at it.

"They used to run tourist trips down here," Peter said, as an explanation. "Then everything was abandoned when the demand stopped."

"Not my idea of a great holiday," Conner muttered.

"We can row it to the *Arc* from here," Peter said. Carefully they got into the old boat and untied it from the jetty.

"This won't sink will it?" Conner asked.

"You can't swim?" Peter replied.

"Not in sewage water no."

"Let's go," Peter said and he took the oars for the boat and started rowing.

The ride was abysmally slow.

"We need to speed this up," Conner said.

He raised his spear and shot a length of energy rope down the tunnel until it stopped extending.

"What are you doing?" Peter said.

Conner didn't answer and just braced himself in the boat.

"Reeling us in," he said and made his spear retract the energy rope. The boat rocketed up the tunnel, pulled by the shrinking rope.

Peter cried out in shock as the boat bounced on the water.

"We'll be there in no time at all," Conner said.

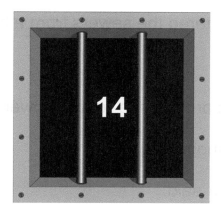

THE LEAFY STAIRWAY

Conner performed his rope trick half a dozen

more times until they were all, according to

Peter, underneath the *Arc de Triomphe*.

They docked the boat at another jetty right next

to a stairwell under the *Arc*.

"What are those?" Peter said pointing at cables

that snaked all the way up to the stairwell.

The wires entered the sewers from a hole in the wall.

"Someone's probably re-routed power to the *Arc*," Elise suggested.

"Why?" Peter said.

Conner shrugged.

They stepped off the boat onto the jetty and Conner shone the light from his spear onto the stairwell.

He paused when he saw what his spear illuminated.

On every flight of steps there was a bulbous plant waiting for them. They looked like Conner's spear. They had long thin stalks with an orb at the end. Unlike Conner's staff though their stalks weren't straight, they twisted about.

As soon as Conner's light shone on them all the plants in the stairwell started homing in on him.

"What are they doing?" Conner asked.

The nearest orbs drew closer and closer to them and suddenly opened up revealing a mouth full of spiny teeth.

"Turn the spear off," Peter said.

"What?"

"Turn the spear off," Peter hissed.

"But we won't be able to see."

"TURN THE SPEAR OFF," Peter shouted.

Conner willed the spear to go dark.

The sewer jetty and stairwell went pitch black.

Conner waited for the plants to guzzle him up and he was even more terrified that he couldn't see it about to do so.

However he wasn't eaten instead he heard the plant move away back to the stairwell.

When he was sure nothing was going to eat him Conner said, "how did you know they wouldn't eat us?"

"They're plants, they don't have eyes, but they can sense light and move towards it," Peter's voice said from the darkness.

"And they were attracted to the light from Conner's staff," Elise concluded.

"Exactly," Peter said.

"So we have to climb the stairs in the dark?" Elise said.

"Yes we do," Peter replied, "try not to touch the plants either or at least not more than once," he added.

"Why?" Conner and Elise asked together.

"I saw some long hairs on the those plants, they are most likely sensors, if you touch them more than once in quick succession the plant will go for you, like a Venus Fly Trap."

"Ok, let's go," Conner said.

Conner led the way in the darkness or he assumed that he was leading the way. He stuck his arms out and tried to remember where the hand rail for the stairs was, then he could use that to climb the stairs and avoid the plants. He breathed a sigh of relief when his hands touched the cold metal rail before they touched the plants.

"I've got the hand rail," Conner whispered.

"I beat you too it," Peter whispered back and Conner could tell that he was above him, already ascending the flight of steps.

"Why are you whispering?" Elise said from behind Conner, "plants don't have ears."

"It just seemed to be the right thing to do," Conner said.

"Get a move on," Elise ordered.

The trio gingerly ascended the stairs. Conner could only see darker shapes moving in the gloom, betraying the presence of the plants that were waiting for them.

"Keep going, as long as there's no light they can't find us," Peter said.

"We need the light too," Conner said.

"Not right now we don't," Peter replied.

●

Above them Luke patrolled the main lobby of the Arc. He stroked the plant he held in his hands and it made cute noises as if it was a little dog. He then admired the plants and flowers that had taken over the building. One of them held a man dressed in the uniform of a security guard. He was suspended from multiple vines and he wasn't awake.

He then gazed at Kutterwood who was doing something with the power cables he had brought to her.

"So what are they for anyway?" he said to Kutterwood.

Her vines were re-linking the cables into a plant she had grown in the centre of the room. It was basically a fat cactus with a basin on top and no spines.

"It a power converter," Kutterwood replied.

"It's a cactus," Luke replied.

"No it's a power converter," Kutterwood said irritably.

"What does it do?"

"It will channel all the power in the city into this,"
Kutterwood said and opened her mouth and spat
out a small round object, it matched the basin on
the cactus perfectly. Kutterwood lifted the sphere
to the cactus.

"Once the power converter has drained the city
of all its electricity it will activate this and the city
will be mine, my greatest stolen treasure."

"What's it called?" Luke said.

"It's called - the Torpor Contain," she replied.

THE CALL

After some careful climbing Conner, Elise and

Peter made it to the top of the stairwell where

there was a cold steel door.

It was still pitch black where they were, but

Conner knew they were all present, he could

hear their nervous breathing.

Fortunately they had not disturbed any of the

plants on their way up.

"Right when we go through this door there will be some light, so we have to get through quick, or the plants will get us," Conner said.

The darker shapes that were Elise and Peter seemed to nod.

"I can't see you nodding," Conner said.

"Oh yeah," Elise and Peter said together.

"Is everyone ready?" he asked.

"Yes," was the reply from both of them.

It was then that weirdly, a tune started playing. The music was coming from Peter. "Sorry it's my phone, probably my mum." The French boy took the phone out of his pocket and tapped it. His face lit up as the screen came on from its standby mode.

"Is that a new *smartphone*?" Conner asked, craning to have a look at the screen over Peter's shoulder.

"Turn it off," Elise said.

"Yes it is," Peter smiled.

"I really want one of those," Conner said.

"YOU IDIOTS TURN THAT OFF NOW," Elise screamed at them, but it was too late. Attracted by the new light source the plants homed in on them. Appearing out of the gloom came several mouths all biting and chomping. Conner struggled with the door desperate to get it open and flee from the hungry plants.

THE THEFT

Peter pulled out a bottle and he started spraying.

The weed killer instantly destroyed the plants

which withered and shrunk away from the spray.

Elise raised her shield and deflected one of the

plants while another bit down on the shield

grasping it between its teeth. Elise willed it to

produce a bubble of energy and as the bubble

expanded the plant's mouth was forced open and ripped apart.

Conner finally got the door open and the trio spilled out into the lobby of the *Arc*.

They were dazzled by the abundance of light in the lobby. The plants on the stairs were attracted to it instantly, following them through the door.

Peter, the last through, sprayed the nearest plant then kicked the door shut behind them.

They all lay on the leaf covered floor of the building, gasping for breath.

"Hi guys," Luke said.

Luke was a few feet away pointing a weird plant at them. Behind him, Conner and Elise recognised Kutterwood, Peter pointed at the plant and his mouth opened and closed without sound. Words failed him, he could not express what he was seeing.

Luke fired the plant he held and the Venus Fly Trap like mouth shot at Peter and it grasped the bottle he held in his left hand. The mouth then retracted back to Luke who fished the bottle out of its jaws. Peter went for his other bottle but Luke fired again and stole that one too.

"We can't have you ruining everything with that weed killer," Kutterwood said.

A football sized seed grew from Kutterwood and enclosed the bottles in a hardened shell.

"They can't hurt me in there," Kutterwood said, then rolled the seed away into the corner of the room.

"Why are you here in this city Kutterwood?" Conner asked, amazed and entranced by the alien's appearance, while at the same time angry that she was no doubt about to perform some crime against humanity.

"I intend to steal this city," she announced.

"Why?" Elise asked getting up off the floor.

"Why? Why? Because I like beautiful and rare things - rare and shiny things. Everything I want must be mine. Once this city is completely sealed off I'll have jewels, artwork and architecture to treasure forever."

"How are you going to steal this city," Peter said.

"And seal it off?" Conner added.

"With this," Kutterwood stated, revealing the Torpor Contain on its cactus pillar.

"What's that?" Conner asked.

"The Torpor Contain, an inescapable prison which I will use to encompass this city and keep it with me for as long as I shall live," Kutterwood said.

"How?" Elise asked.

"Once the Contain has enough power it will grow to a diameter of ten miles and then its walls will solidify and prevent anything from leaving and anything from entering. "I will have it all to myself."

THE PRISON

"Ok," Conner said and he fired a net from his spear straight at Kutterwood.

The net widened and enveloped her, wrapping up her vines and constricting her body.

"Elise get the Contain, Peter get your bottles we're going to need them," Conner ordered.

Luke stepped forward and fired his plant at Conner's spear and the Thorn Wire's mouth bit on the shaft of the weapon.

Luke then pulled on the stem of the plant he held, but Conner maintained his grip on the spear and he and Luke started a tug-of-war match.

"Let go mate," Conner said, straining against his friends strength.

"Can you let go please?" Luke asked.

"Come on mate fight that brainwashing, you don't want to do this do you?" Conner said.

"I'm afraid the brainwashing was quite good I cannot stop," Luke replied as calmly as a monk,

and continued trying to take the spear from
Conner.

●

Elise made it to the cactus in the centre of the
room. It appeared to be pulsating with energy.
She wondered whether or not she should
remove the power cables, but then realised she
might electrocute herself.

She studied the Torpor Contain. It was basically
a small sphere with two dials on its surface. Two
symbols were etched into it. One was a circle
within a circle, with arrows highlighting the
difference in size. Elise assumed that was a
setting for the width of the force-field, just like
Mach had said. The other symbol was basically

a clock and Elise concluded that whatever you set it to was the length of time the prison was sealed for, again like Mach had described.

"Stay away from that," Kutterwood screamed. She was still trapped inside her net, but she was poking her vines through the gaps and extending them to reach out for Elise.

Elise raised her shield to block the alien's attack. The shield held against the alien. Elise realised that she could never beat Kutterwood like this, she needed a new strategy.

•

Peter crawled over to the seed that contained his weed killer.

He tried to pound it with his fists but the seed did not relent against his attacks.

He picked it up and slammed it on the ground. It refused to break.

He looked around for something to pierce it. With all this giant alien plant life around he hoped to find a large thorn, but there wasn't anything like that.

Instead he saw numerous plants suddenly detach themselves from the wall and use their roots to walk towards him. They were just like the plants he, Conner and Elise had fought in the darkness, except these had eyes and they were completely focused on Peter.

Then he heard someone groan. It was a man in a uniform, a guard for the *Arc* no doubt, and he was hanging from the wall amongst a bunch of vines. Peter saw a nightstick dangling in the plants beside him. He rushed over pulled the stick from the vines that held it and dug the weapon into the seed.

The tough metal tube went right in and Peter twisted it and split the seed.

The plants were inches away and he didn't have time to lever the seed open.

The nearest plant shot forward with an open mouth. Peter had only one thing with which to shield himself from the attack, and raised the seed pod. The plant's jaws bit down on the seed and shattered it between its teeth.

Peter's weed killer bottles dropped to the floor and he scooped them up. He immediately started spraying dispatching any plant that came close.

He twirled on the spot as the plants surrounded and dived towards him. They received a spray of weed killer in their faces for their trouble.

Eventually Peter stood alone surrounded by twitching and decaying plants.

He would have yelled in triumph, however he saw the trouble Elise was in.

●

Elise's shield was grabbed by the vines of Kutterwood and prised from her grip.

"Now you're the only thing in my way," Kutterwood said.

Elise cringed away from the vines that swooped in to attack her.

Peter however barged her aside and started spraying.

A cloud of weed killer spread out from him and as soon as the vines touched it they withered and dried up.

Kutterwood screamed in pain as Peter continued to spit weed killer at her and she backed away.

Elise used the distraction and reached out for the Torpor Contain.

"No," Kutterwood yelled and she suddenly flayed her vines everywhere and struck her and Peter, throwing them away from the cactus/power converter.

Elise barely had her hands on it for a few seconds before she was pushed aside, now it was out of her reach completely.

The cactus the Contain sat on stopped pulsating and it started to flash on and off, emitting a green light.

"It's ready," Kutterwood said in joy and she walked over to the cactus and plucked the Contain from its place.

"Now you and this city are mine forever and when you're sealed in this Contain with me you will all become my slaves."

Luke and Conner stopped their struggle and turned to watch.

"Time to go," Luke said and he let go of his Thorn Wire and reached into his pocket. "You'll need this, it's Kutterwood teleporter," he said, and chucked a small sphere to Conner.

"What?" Conner said his mind not catching up fast enough, causing him to fumble with the sphere.

Luke then held out his own teleporter taken from Snorflag.

"No Luke, no," Conner called out, but it was too late Luke's teleporter took him away.

Kutterwood laughed and laughed as the Torpor Contain's flashing increased in speed. It was only seconds away from activating.

"My greatest theft," Kutterwood boasted and she raised her floral limbs into the air in triumph.

The Torpor Contain emitted a bubble from its surface that enveloped Kutterwood.

Her laughter was silenced as the sphere overcame her.

Conner and Peter stepped away expecting it to envelope them too, however instead the Contain remained as it was and didn't grow larger.

Kutterwood's laughter could not be heard from inside the Contain, but after a few seconds they did hear her start banging on the inside of the sphere. Faintly they heard Kutterwood scream, "LET ME OUT," from inside. However her voice was extremely muffled.

"I don't get it, Mach said the Contain could be miles in diameter," Conner said.

"Not if you set it to a smaller size," Elise grinned. "I set the Contain on its lowest setting, which is only big enough for Kutterwood," she added indicating the sphere. "Now the only treasure she has is herself."

"Practically worthless then," Peter said.

"Good one," Conner laughed.

"We did it," Conner said and held out his hands for high fives, which he received.

"Hey Look," Elise said pointing at the vines and plants around them.

Conner and Peter looked and saw that everything was turning brown and dying.

"I guess without Kutterwood it can't live," Elise commented.

"Let's get her back to Mach's ship," Conner said as the dying plant life rained down on them.

"Is that it?" Peter said.

"Yeah that's it," Conner replied, "job done, the world is safe once again. Thank you for your help Peter and I'm sorry I shot those nets at you," Conner apologised.

"No problem, thank you for dealing with the invaders," he said.

"We'll see you around," Conner remarked.

"You'd better," Peter shot back smiling.

Conner placed his hand on the surface of the Contain. He activated the teleporter Luke had given him and Peter watched them disappear.

He looked around the *Arc* that was being freed of plant life; he wondered if the rest of Paris was also being liberated in the same manner.

As he looked around he spotted a plant that was still green and not dying.

He recognised it as the weapon the boy called Luke had been carrying.

He picked it up and took it with him as he left.

18

THE EXCUSE

Mach was pleased that they had caught Kutterwood and imprisoned her in the Torpor Contain. She was even more secure inside that thing than she had been in her cell in the prison ship.

Conner didn't stay for the celebrations. After the alien had been returned to her cell he moped off.

Elise had sensed how troubled he was feeling and let him go.

During the walk back Conner noticed that the forest was in fall and the leaves were falling like rain.

The beautiful autumn scene made him moody and angry.

He wanted to forget about Paris, but the wildlife around him kept his thoughts in that city. He couldn't stop thinking of his best friend who he had come so close to helping and yet he had let slip through his fingers.

He had failed to get Luke back home safely, again.

For a second he almost fell into a deep depression at the thought of his friend being still out there, helping another alien to endanger the planet Earth.

But there was something about their encounter that made Conner realise that maybe it wasn't as bad as it seemed.

Luke, the Luke he knew, was still in there somewhere. Despite Snorflag's brainwashing Luke remembered who Conner was and talked to him like a friend. He had also handed him that teleporter so that they could have escaped the Contain if necessary.

Conner left the forest and entered his back garden he smiled slightly, Luke was safe and because of that he should be thankful.

His hand reached out for the back door of his house and instead his mother opened it for him and glared down at him.

"You've been out in that forest for ages," his mother complained.

"Sorry mum," Conner replied and he walked under her arm and entered the house.

"You can't just rush out after school like that, don't you have homework to do?" his mother declared.

Conner picked up a nearby piece of paper sitting on the kitchen table and then brought out Mach's Disguise Spray from his pocket.

He sent two puffs into the air then handed the piece of paper to his mum.

"Here's my homework," he said.

His mother took the paper and looked at it.

"Sorrrrry hooooooney," she said staring at the blank piece of paper.

"You caaaaan goooo into the forest whenever yoooou want - as long as it's always done," she said.

"No problem mum," Conner replied. He then headed upstairs to do his homework for real.

THE END

JOIN CONNER, ELISE AND LUKE ON THE

NEXT HUNT

WHO IS THE ALIEN THEY ARE AFTER?

THE MALEVOLENT CREATURE KNOWN AS...

GLAYCIAR OF EYCE

WATCH OUT HE'S **COLD**

BLOODED

PROLOGUE

Los Angeles, the city of Angels.

At the moment the city was experiencing a heat wave.

The air was dry and made anyone who dared venture outside hot and sweaty.

It was odd then that a pond in the city centre was currently completely frozen over.

Scientists from the nearby weather centre were at a loss as to how to explain this bizarre phenomenon.

Lots of news reporters were at the scene commenting on it, giving up-to-date information on TV and the internet. It was also in all the morning papers.

At the scene was Lisa Hooper reporting for NEPCC, the largest news corporation in the city.

"I'm here at the Watercourt on Bunker Hill in the historic core of the city, and as you can see the pool is completely frozen over. Even the waterfalls are solid giving us this eerie spectacle," she said, beginning her broadcast.

She then listened to a question in her ear piece from a colleague in the studio.

"Yes Phil, scientists don't know how this has happened, as you know it's a scorching 35 degrees in Los Angeles today and the formation of ice is baffling experts."

She listened to another comment.

"Yes, yes we will stay here and keep you updated," she said.

The cameraman then said "cut," and she was off the air.

Lisa fumed where she stood.

"What a rubbish story," she said to the cameraman.

"I know all I've got is an hour's footage of just ice," he said. "Someone should at least chuck a penguin on it to give it some character."

"I thought this was going to be big news," Lisa said.

"So did I," the cameraman agreed. "I thought a natural disaster was going to take place, like in that film," he suggested.

Lisa Hooper had also been thinking that. It was interesting that ice had formed in this pond, but also boring in that there appeared to be no explanation, so the story went nowhere.

"Hey kid get off there would you," a cop suddenly shouted.

Lisa looked out across the pond and saw that a young, blond boy was walking across the ice to the centre of the pond without a care that it was likely to crack under his weight.

She watched a cop get up onto the ice and follow the child, waving his hands and shouting. He was unsteady on the slippery ice, while the boy suffered no difficulty. The boy looked perfectly normal; a regular child except that he wore some strange gauntlets on his arms. He was so casual it looked like he was just out for a stroll. Lisa assumed that he was doing it as a bet.

"Bill start rolling," Lisa said hoping that whatever the boy was doing was going somewhere interesting.

The camera started filming.

The boy reached the centre of the pond knelt down and pulled a stone from his pocket.

For some reason he bashed on the ice with the stone in a repeating pattern, as if doing Morse code.

The cop reached the boy just as he finished his message.

"Come with me son," the cop said and reached out to grab the boy's shoulder.

The boy moved out from under the cop's hand at astonishing speed and walked away towards the edge of the pond.

"I've just woken him, it would be best if you got off the ice," the boy said over his shoulder.

The cop decided to run after the kid, which was difficult because of the slippy-ness of the ground he was on. Eventually though he caught up with the boy at the edge of the pond.

"Stop, boy stop," the cop ordered.

It was then that the pond ice cracked. The policeman was unbalanced as the ice he stood on slid and shifted.

Out of the icy pond a giant hairy beast erupted from the frozen water. It was followed by several smaller hairy beasts.

Everyone nearby started screaming, chunks of ice rained down all around the pond. As the ice broke apart the cracking sounds it made were deafening.

The boy stepped off what remained of the ice and turned to look at his latest master.

"I've found what you wanted," he said loudly in order to be heard.

"Good," the hairy beast replied. "Time to put this planet on a diet."

The boy disappeared in a flash of light and from the hairy beast a wave of ice flowed across the city freezing everything in its path.

Lisa Hooper and her cameraman ran for their lives.